Little Blossom Stories

Ella Plans a Garden

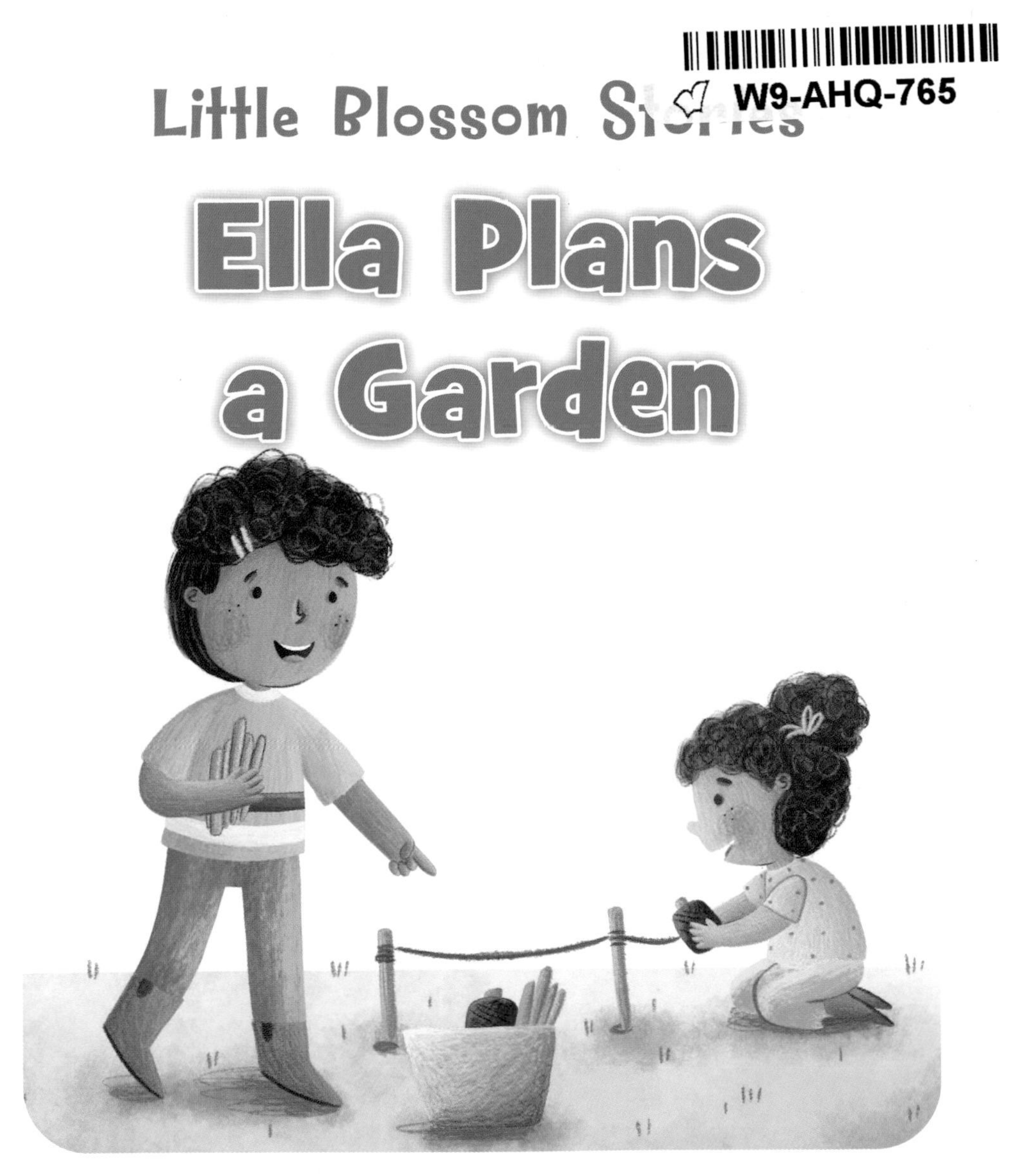

By Cecilia Minden

Ella wants a garden.

"I want a garden just for me."

"Mom, will you help me
plan a garden?"

"I will help you plan
a garden, Ella."

"Let us look for a good spot."

Ella and Mom look for a good spot.

"We need a spot with lots of sun."

"This spot has lots of sun."

"This is a good spot
for a garden."

"This is a good spot for a
garden just for me."

"What will you put in
your garden, Ella?"

What can Ella put in her garden?

sight words

a
for
garden
good
help
her
I
look
me
need
of
want
wants
We
What
you
your

short a words	short e words	short i words	short o words	short u words
can	Ella	in	lots	just
has	Let	is	Mom	put
plan		This	spot	sun
		will		us
		with		

90 Words

Ella wants a garden.
"I want a garden just for me."
"Mom, will you help me plan a garden?"
"I will help you plan a garden, Ella."
"Let us look for a good spot."
Ella and Mom look for a good spot.
"We need a spot with lots of sun."
"This spot has lots of sun."
"This is a good spot for a garden."
"This is a good spot for a garden just for me."
"What will you put in your garden, Ella?'
What can Ella put in her garden?

Published in the United States of America by Cherry Lake Publishing Group
Ann Arbor, Michigan
www.cherrylakepublishing.com

Illustrator: Megan Higgins

Cherry Blossom Press is an imprint of Cherry Lake Publishing Group.

Library of Congress Cataloging-in-Publication Data

Names: Minden, Cecilia, author. | Higgins, Megan, illustrator.
Title: Ella plans a garden / by Cecilia Minden ; illustrated by Megan Higgins.
Description: Ann Arbor, Michigan : Cherry Lake Publishing, 2021. | Series: Little blossom stories | Audience: Grades K-1. | Summary: "Ella decides she wants a garden just for her. This A-level story uses decodable text to raise confidence in early readers. The book uses a combination of sight words and short-vowel words in repetition to build recognition. Original illustrations help guide readers through the text"– Provided by publisher.
Identifiers: LCCN 2021005074 (print) | LCCN 2021005075 (ebook) | ISBN 9781534188068 (paperback) | ISBN 9781534189461 (pdf) | ISBN 9781534190863 (ebook)
Subjects: LCSH: Readers (Primary) | Gardens–Juvenile fiction.
Classification: LCC PE1119.2 .M56355 2021 (print) | LCC PE1119.2 (ebook) | DDC 428.6/2–dc23
LC record available at https://lccn.loc.gov/2021005074
LC ebook record available at https://lccn.loc.gov/2021005075

Printed in the United States of America
Corporate Graphics

Cecilia Minden is the former director of the Language and Literacy Program at Harvard Graduate School of Education. She earned her PhD in Reading Education at the University of Virginia. Dr. Minden has written extensively for early readers. She is passionate about matching children to the very book they need to improve their skills and progress to a deeper understanding of all the wonder books can hold.